THE BROCKENSPECTRE

THE BROCKENSPECTRE

Linda Newbery
Illustrated by Pam Smy

CORGI YEARLING

CORGI YEARLING

UK | USA | Canada | Ireland | Australia
India | New Zealand | South Africa

Corgi Yearling is part of the Penguin Random House group of companies
whose addresses can be found at global.penguinrandomhouse.com.

www.penguin.co.uk
www.puffin.co.uk
www.ladybird.co.uk

Penguin
Random House
UK

First Jonathan Cape edition published 2014
This edition published 2017

001

Typeset in ITC New Baskerville
Printed in Great Britain by Clays Ltd, St Ives plc

A CIP catalogue record for this book is available from the British Library

ISBN: 978–0–440–87114–9

All correspondence to
Corgi Yearling
Penguin Random House Children's
80 Strand, London WC2R 0RL

*For Dad, who told me about them many years ago,
and for Pam, the most gifted and generous of illustrators*

CONTENTS

THE BROCKENSPECTRE

Part One

Pappi

Oh yes, boy, I've seen the Brockenspectre. When I'm up high, and alone. He waits. He chooses his moment.

No, it's no use running away. He goes with you. You might think you only imagined him, but you didn't. He's there, waiting. And you keep going back, because you have to. The mountains won't let you go, once you're under their spell.

The mountains are a dream you have to follow, or spend your life regretting it.

What's he like? Oh – huge. Dark. A giant made of shadow.

Am I frightened? No. I don't talk about fear, boy. Don't even think of it. Fear is no use to a mountain climber. Fear can freeze your blood and numb your mind. Fear everything, and you'll do nothing.

Chapter One:

Niklas Rust

Tomas's father was a big, handsome man. His fair hair grew thick and straight, and his blond beard was neatly trimmed. His eyes were blue – a clear, startling blue – and his face was tanned by the sun and the wind. His strong legs could carry him all day long without tiring. With his fairness and the blue of his eyes, Mamma said he was like bright sunshine in May.

He was Niklas Rust.

Mamma said that she'd fallen in love the very first time she saw him striding down the hillside, one afternoon in autumn with low sun behind him.

Tomas was like him, people said, but when Tomas looked in the mirror he saw that his eyes weren't as blue nor his hair as fair as his father's. Still, there was *something* of Pappi in the face that gazed back. It made him proud to think so.

Pappi was a mountain guide. The peaks and valleys of the Alps drew people from far away, to walk, climb and explore. They came by railway train to the city down by the lake, and up the winding road to the village by pony trap. They came from France and from Italy, from Austria and from England, and from even farther places. They stayed at the Alpenrose Inn in the village, where Tomas's friend Karl lived, and Pappi was paid to lead them up to the summits and the high passes. But his work also took him to other villages and towns that attracted mountain climbers. It wasn't unusual for him to be away for a month at a time, and that made his stays at home very special.

Whenever Pappi wasn't in the mountains he was getting ready to go again. He would clean his boots, pack his sturdy rucksack, check that he had his whistle and his compass and his rope. In the morning he'd call goodbye in the cheery way he had, eager to be gone.

Often it seemed that he was away more than he was at home, and Tomas

knew that this made his mother sad. She looked forward to his coming back – they all did. The house felt so different when Pappi was with them.

They were never sure when he'd come. For days and weeks at a time his work took him away. Then, some time when they weren't expecting him, he'd be there, shouting, 'Hello! I'm home!' Little Johanna would run to him, and he'd lift her high in his arms. He filled the house with his big voice and his big presence.

There were four of them in the family: Mamma and Pappi, Tomas and Johanna. On days when Pappi stayed at home, he made wooden chairs, stools and window boxes in the workshop outside, for Mamma to paint. She decorated them with flowers and alpine scenes, and displayed them for sale outside the cottage. They were bought by visitors to the village, who liked to have something from the Alps to keep.

Mamma took great care with her pictures, and they were admired by everyone who saw them. With the money she made, and Pappi's earnings from mountain guiding, there was just about enough for the family.

Tomas liked painting, too, but he wasn't good enough yet to paint scenes for Mamma to sell. Practising on a small offcut, he painted a raven on a rocky crag, with blue sky behind.

He was pleased with that, and gave it to Pappi. Pappi held it in his hand, examining it.

'Taking after your mother, are you?' he said. 'I was hoping to make a mountaineer of you.'

Then he left it on the workbench when he went indoors for supper.

Chapter Two:
Johanna's Birthday

It was Johanna's second birthday. There was a special tea at Nanni's house.

Nanni had made a marvellous cake with two candles. The table was set and the lamps were lit. Johanna wore a new dress Mamma had embroidered for her. Nanni and Mamma had put on their best skirts and blouses, and Tomas had polished his shoes.

The only thing missing was Pappi.

'He promised to be here,' Mamma kept saying. 'I'm sure he'll come soon.'

Nanni kept glancing at the clock on the mantelpiece. Occasionally she made a small sound: '*Tchh!*'

Johanna played on the rug with her new bear, but no one else looked happy. Mamma was trying to be cheerful, and failing. Tomas tried to join in Johanna's game of pretend. But he sensed that harsh words were hovering on his grandmother's tongue. At last she spat them out.

'That man of yours!' she accused Mamma, as if it was her fault that Pappi wasn't here. 'Where is he this time? You can't rely on him. Wouldn't you think he'd make an effort to be here?'

'Now, Mother, that's not fair,' said Mamma. 'Niklas will come, I'm sure he will. Something's held him up.'

'Oh yes, something, something! Something more important than his own darling girl! Poor little Johanna. On her *birthday*. Well, I'm not waiting any longer. We'll have tea.'

It felt wrong to start the birthday tea with Mamma and Nanni wearing bright, false smiles. The cake Nanni had made was iced with flowers, and was easily big enough for ten people. It sat in splendour in the middle of the table, defying anyone to touch it. Nanni passed a plate of fruit bread, and Tomas took a slice. His stomach rumbled emptily but he didn't feel like eating.

Then there came a loud rapping on the door. Pappi was here.

'Sorry – sorry for being late!'

He was a gust of mountain air, blowing away the bad feeling. His laugh rippled as he scooped Johanna into his arms and lifted her high above his head, making her squeal and pretend to be frightened.

'One of my climbers twisted an ankle, and held us all up. Happy birthday, little Jo! Yes, yes, little sweetheart, Pappi's here. I wouldn't miss your birthday, would I? Oh, what a wonderful cake Nanni's made for you! Isn't she a good granny?'

Tomas was so pleased to have Pappi at home
that he kept talking about it at school.

Franz Goll was scornful.

'*Pappi, Pappi, Pappi!*' he mocked, as they
collected their coats at the end of the day.
'What's so wonderful about that pappi of yours?
Anyone can do what he does.'

That was ridiculous! Tomas laughed. 'Anyone
can't!'

'They can. My Onkel Philipp's a better
mountaineer than your precious pappi.'

'No he isn't.'

'Yes he is. Onkel Philipp's been up the
Schritterhorn, twice.'

'So what? My father's climbed it four times.'

Franz jutted his chin. 'Onkel Philipp's been
up all the highest peaks, not just ours. He's
been up mountains in France. And in Austria.
And in Italy. Even in Spain. What's your pappi
done that's so marvellous?'

'He's been up more mountains than I know
the names of,' Tomas told him. 'Some with

names I can't even pronounce.'

'Anyone can say that. How d'you know he's not making it up?'

'He's seen the – the Brockenspectre,' Tomas flung back. Even to say the word sent a shiver down his back.

'The what?'

'The Brockenspectre. Haven't you heard of it? A huge, fearsome mountain ghost. So your uncle doesn't know everything, then?'

'He could have seen it! I bet he has.'

Tomas shook his head. 'He'd have been terrified solid if he had.'

'He wouldn't. Not Onkel Philipp.'

'And,' said Tomas, 'what about all the people my dad's saved? He's gone out after people lost in the snow, and brought them back. Lots of times.'

'They've got a big dog up at the monastery that does that. Seek, they say, and it goes trotting off. P'raps we should give your pappi a new name – Saint Bernard!'

Franz was so pleased with his joke that he

told his friend Peter. As they went out of the school gates and along the lane, he and Peter kept shoving each other, and shouting 'Saint Bernard! Sit! Good dog!' and whuffing and barking.

'Don't take any notice,' said Tomas's friend Karl. 'Franz is just jealous, 'cos his dad's old and fat. I bet he wishes he had a dad like yours.'

Tomas was proud of Pappi. Of course he was. Pappi was so strong, and so brave. He had travelled so far, and seen so much. He wasn't afraid of the sheerest heights. He wasn't afraid of slinking wolves. Even the Brockenspectre couldn't really scare him. Not Pappi.

Chapter Three:
Together

Pappi and Tomas went out walking on the lower slopes. They followed a track that led up beside the Schneegletscher, the broad glacier that swept down between stands of pine and fir. The river of ice reached almost as far as the village. Tomas gazed at the frozen glide, and the blue depths.

Walks like this were special. Just him and Pappi, together.

Pappi told him that the glaciers, over hundreds of thousands of years, had carved out the valleys. They had made the green meadows that were bright with flowers through the spring and summer, grazed by cows and goats. Ice carving rock! It seemed impossible. Tomas would have thought that rock was stronger than anything.

He wanted to cross the ice river to the other side, but Pappi stopped him.

'Don't take chances with glaciers, boy. Don't ever walk across. There are crevasses, deeper than you'd think. You might slip through, and never get out. Bodies have been found, years and years later.'

Tomas shivered. He imagined someone trapped in ice, cold and still as a princess in a fairy tale.

But no kiss in the world could bring life to that frozen body.

'You must respect the mountain,' Pappi said. 'Don't try to beat it. The mountain always wins. Don't ever forget that.'

Mamma was happy to have Pappi at home, and cooked his favourite meals, and darned and mended his shirts and his socks.

Soon, though, being at home and working in the woodshed made Pappi restless. He loved the mountains best. Most of all, he loved being in the mountains alone.

In the woodshed, he was a quick and impatient worker, not like Mamma, who took endless care with her pictures of flowers and snow-capped mountains. He annoyed her by putting on his boots and going out, leaving his woodwork half finished and the shed in a mess.

After a few days of this, Pappi was hired to take out groups from the Alpenrose Inn, every day for a week.

But even Pappi's guiding work could make him cross. To earn money he had to take anyone who'd pay. Not all of them were good climbers. Some were hopeless.

'What's the matter with them?' he complained.

Mamma had cooked pork sausages, his favourite, but he ate them without noticing. 'These people who moan about blisters after half a day. Or the ones with no head for heights, who get scared when they look down. Idiots. What do they expect, up a mountain?'

'You must be patient, Niklas,' Mamma told him. 'They pay your wages.'

But Pappi was not patient. Tomas knew that.

What Pappi really liked, when he'd made enough stools and window boxes to keep Mamma busy with her painting, was to go off alone for a week or more. He'd cross the mountains into the next valley, or stay high on the ridge, sleeping under the stars or in one of the refuge huts.

Tomas wanted to go, but Pappi said that it was too far and too hard. 'When you're older,' he promised. 'When you're stronger. Maybe then I'll take you with me.' And off he'd go, whistling.

And Tomas knew that he really preferred to be on his own.

'It's as if I've only got half a husband,' Mamma had complained to Pappi once. 'Only half of you is here. The other half belongs to the mountains.'

Pappi tossed his head. 'Don't nag me, woman. You've known that from the start. Why expect anything different?'

At school, Fräulein Glockner was telling the class the story of Wilhelm Tell.

They already knew it, of course. Everyone did. Wilhelm Tell was a Swiss hero. Wherever you went, there were plaques and statues and carvings of Wilhelm Tell with his bow and arrow. Today, Fräulein wanted each of the children to write part of the story, and to draw a picture. She planned to make a frieze for the classroom wall.

Whenever Tomas heard the story – at first told by Mamma, later reading it himself in a book – he pictured Wilhelm Tell as tall and strong, with straight fair hair, a neat beard and bright blue eyes. He looked just like Pappi.

And there was Wilhelm's son, Walter, who faced terrible danger without flinching. That was the part of the story Tomas chose to write about: how the cruel Austrian governor condemned father and son to death, then offered them one chance to save themselves. But the chance was a very dangerous one. An apple was placed on Walter's head, and Wilhelm Tell had to pierce it by firing an arrow from his crossbow. Wilhelm Tell was a skilled marksman – but if he missed he might kill his own son in a horrible way. Yet if he refused to try, they'd both die anyway.

Bending over his paper and pencil, concentrating hard, Tomas imagined himself as Walter – every inch of him trying to balance the apple on his head, keeping himself straight and steady. Trusting his father with all his might.

Chapter Four:

Gone

It was a bad start to the day.

Sleety rain had kept Pappi indoors for nearly
a week. He was supposed to guide a group from
the inn for a whole week's climbing, but there
was flooding down in the valley, the trains were
delayed, and the guests couldn't reach the
village. On the third day, Karl's father, Herr
Donders, came to the cottage with a letter to

show Pappi. The climbers had decided to put off their tour until the spring.

That meant Pappi would lose a whole week's pay. So no money would come in at all. Mamma hadn't sold a single stool or window box, and wasn't likely to, with no visitors in the village.

When Pappi was in a bad mood, he was a different person. His face darkened. His eyebrows were drawn so low that you couldn't see the blue of his eyes. He couldn't settle, and his pacing up and down made everyone restless.

'Another wet day! When will it end?'

'Sit down, Niklas, and eat your breakfast.' Mamma passed him a bowl of porridge. There was soft new bread, too, and creamy butter, and honey. But Pappi might as well have been gnawing at a raw turnip.

Mamma tried again. 'You could go out to the workshop when you've finished?'

'I've spent hours and hours in that blasted workshop!' Pappi raged. 'I'm sick of the sight of it. It's not as if anyone wants to buy your painted knick-knackery!' He waved an arm at the door. 'Can you see customers queuing?'

'Niklas, you know we don't sell much in winter! But we need to be ready for next year. Have a bit of sense!'

'*You* show some sense, woman!'

Tomas hated it when his parents argued. He wanted everything to be perfect when Pappi was home.

Quarrels like this made him feel that everything was wrong.

Mamma pressed her lips together, and said no more. Johanna, in her high chair, started to cry – the miserable, grizzling kind of crying that only made Pappi crosser.

'Shh, shh, little Jo!' Tomas got up from his chair and lifted Johanna out of hers, cuddling and soothing. She cuddled him back, and stopped crying. She loved her big brother.

'Don't, Tom,' Pappi grumped, head down. 'She's not a baby any more. Don't treat her like one. She must sit and eat her breakfast without screaming for attention.'

The kettle was boiling, with a long, rising shriek.

'Oh, Niklas – you and your bad moods!'
Mamma got up to pour water on the coffee.
'Tommi's only trying to help! Do you want
everyone to be as bad-tempered as you are?'

'All right. All *right*!' Pappi looked up. 'Enough
of your nagging. I'll walk as far as school with
you, boy. I need to get out of the house.'

'Good. Try to come back in a better mood,'
Mamma chided.

Tomas had listened, and watched, and felt
uneasy, and now the words burst out of him.
'I don't want you with me,' he told Pappi. 'Not
when you're so grumpy. Why do you have to *be*
like this? I'll walk by myself.'

He'd finished his breakfast. He went out into
the rain to finish his morning jobs: letting the
chickens into the meadow, and putting new
straw in their nest box.

The chickens didn't want to go out in the
rain. They huddled in their house, clucking
irritably. *Everyone* was in a bad mood today.

When Tomas went back indoors, Pappi had
gone.

Supper time came, and Pappi's place at the table stayed empty. Sleet had turned to snow, whiting out the landscape.

'Where did he say he was going?' Tomas asked Mamma.

'He didn't. You know how he is. He just walked out. Didn't even say goodbye.'

She looked so worried that Tomas told her, 'Don't worry! I expect everything will be all right.'

Mamma sighed. 'Yes. Perhaps it will.'

But Tomas saw how she kept watching the door, and how often she glanced out of the window.

Tomas told himself that Pappi would come back tomorrow, as if there'd been no argument. He was like that. His bad tempers disappeared like rainclouds when the sun broke through.

But Pappi didn't turn up the next day. Or the next. Or the next.

*

A week passed.

If Pappi had been any other mountain walker failing to return, search parties would have been sent out that first night, with a dog, lanterns and a warming flask of brandy. But no one had thought of searching for Pappi, because he came and went so often, and stayed away so long, and on purpose.

Tomas kept telling himself that nothing bad could have happened. Pappi knew the mountains in all their moods. He was big and strong, and could walk for miles without tiring.

Pappi didn't know fear. He had said so, often enough.

But . . . but . . .

In bed that seventh night, Tomas couldn't stop thinking about the Brockenspectre.

Pappi said he wasn't scared of it, but what if the Brockenspectre had surprised him? Crept up on him, in the distant heights where Pappi loved to go? Where the cliffs were sheer, dropping to jagged rocks below? What if it had startled him into slipping and falling?

Tomas imagined himself as Pappi – making his way slowly, treading carefully in the fresh snow, head down against the wind. The mountain tops spread all around him like a white wilderness, with no living creature but himself.

But something was up there, something huge and shadowy. Through the blur of his snow-crusted eyelashes, a dark figure swam at him – enormous, with arms held out stiffly . . .

'*No!*' Tomas yelled, and woke himself. He was in his bed tucked under the attic eaves, warm and safe. There was no white-out, no snow, no Brockenspectre. Nearby, in her cot, Johanna was breathing softly, fast asleep.

But he shivered. The dream was real in his mind.

He hadn't seen the creature's face. He didn't want to.

He knew it would be terrible.

It was the Brockenspectre.

PART TWO

Talk

At church, the people said: 'We must keep him in our prayers.'

They said: 'May it please God that he comes back safe and sound.'

They said: 'What will be will be. God rest his soul.'

And someone had heard of a wanderer who was lost for a year and a day. His memory was gone, and he'd survived by living in a cave, like a wild man.

In the Alpenrose Inn, the drinkers said: 'He always was a strange one, that Niklas Rust. Kept himself to himself.'

They said: 'Rust? Niklas Rust? Surefooted as a mountain goat, he was.'

They said: 'One slip, though. One loosened rock. That's all it takes.'

And someone remembered a man who'd climbed all the highest peaks in Europe, but was hit by a falling boulder on the slopes of the Schritterhorn, and fell to his death.

In the village shop, the customers said: 'It's his wife I feel for, poor soul. Left on her own with the two children.'

They said: 'Remember all those old stories. About spirits and spectres and ghasts that wail up there on the high peaks. Who knows what's true and what isn't?'

And someone knew of someone who'd heard of a man lost in the heights and discovered weeks later, solid as ice, his face a frozen mask of horror.

Chapter Five:

The Schritterhorn

Months had gone by. Almost a whole year. It was autumn again, and still there was no news of Pappi. Winter would soon come, and snow would cut the village off from the valley. The high tops would be too dangerous for all but the toughest mountaineers.

Winter, Tomas thought, would bring the end of hoping.

At first, when Johanna asked, 'Where's Pappi?' Mamma would answer, 'He'll be home soon, sweetheart.'

But *soon* became *maybe another week or two*, and then *when it suits him* and *some time – don't worry*. By now *I really don't know* would have been the only reply Mamma could make. Tomas never asked, because he could see that it pained her to answer.

Now that she was the only earner, Mamma had to work hard. In the mornings, every day except Sunday, she did laundry and ironing at the Alpenrose Inn, while Nanni looked after Johanna. In the afternoons and evenings she painted her stools and window boxes to sell. Without Pappi to make them, she had to rely on Max, the village carpenter. The money she paid him meant there was less for the family.

It was bad enough losing Pappi, without

Mamma having to worry about the cost of everything as well. Tomas was growing fast, and needed a new pair of boots and a new jacket,  but where would the money come from?

Since Pappi left, Mamma had been questioning everyone she met. When climbers stayed at the Alpenrose, she asked them to look out for Pappi, and to pass on anything they heard in other villages, or from people they met on the mountain paths. But no news came.

Tomas's chest tightened every time he saw a group of climbers tramping up the steep paths that led out of the village. The groups had to bring their own guides until Karl's father hired someone new; someone good enough.

It should have been Pappi. Pappi was the best guide – everyone knew that.

At home, there was a big gap where Pappi should have been. And a silence, a silence of waiting. A silence in which nothing could really change until Pappi came home, or . . . until they found out what had happened.

Had there been an accident? There were endless ways to have accidents in the mountains. Had Pappi slipped and fallen? Been caught in an avalanche? Something as drastic as that must be the answer . . . *But no, NO*, Tomas thought.

Not Pappi.

Pappi couldn't be . . .

No. Pappi was too big, and strong, and alive, *to be . . .*

Dead was the word Tomas was trying his hardest not to think, even though he knew other people were saying it.

But . . . if Pappi *hadn't* been killed, he was choosing to stay away. And that, too, was horrible to think about.

Pappi's absence was a pain in Tomas's chest. He saw and heard him everywhere he went. Pappi's good moods were more frequent than his glooms, and then everyone was happy. He would laugh uproariously, pretend to be a bear for Johanna, kick a ball around with Tomas and

Karl, and be everything a father should be.

Tomas kept hearing what he'd said to Pappi, that last morning. 'I don't want you with me.'

But he did. He *did.*

Climbing into bed in the attic room he shared with Johanna, Tomas thought of tomorrow. Tomorrow loomed like a marker. It would be a year since Pappi had gone. A whole *year.*

He kept hoping that Pappi would walk through the door as if nothing had happened, as if the year of absence had shrunk to a few days. Tomas hoped and hoped and hoped so. He curled himself into a ball between the cold sheets and gripped his hands into fists, hoping with all his might, his fingernails digging into his palms. *Pappi, come home. Come home tomorrow. Come back to us.*

But an incident after school that day had made hope seem a weak, feeble thing, barely alive.

It was Franz Goll. Of course.

'Your father's still missing, then?' he'd called

41

to Tomas, jostling him as they came outside
into the cold air. 'The mountain ghost got him,
I bet! The gruesome grisly. The spooky spectre.
That's what happened, I bet it did.'

'That's just stupid!' Tomas had yelled back.

But Franz's words had stayed with him.

Now, as he curled up tightly in bed with
his eyes closed, waiting for tomorrow and
what it might bring, there was no escaping
the mountain ghost. It was there in his mind,
waiting till he was too sleepy to push it away.

Then it filled his thoughts, huge and shadowy.

The Brockenspectre followed you. Pappi had said so. Tomas felt as if it was following *him*, though he'd never really seen it.

You couldn't be sure what creatures lived up there in the snowy heights. There were legends. There were stories. Sometimes people saw strange unexplained footprints.

The Brockenspectre was somewhere in the mountains, but also, Tomas knew, it was inside him.

The thought slid into his mind that he wouldn't find Pappi without finding the Brockenspectre as well. It was waiting. And he knew now what it was waiting *for*.

It was waiting for him.

It was waiting to show itself. And it would only do that if he went looking.

He knew from the grey light that it was time to get up. Shivering, he climbed out of bed and pulled open the curtains.

The small window under the roof eaves

looked down on a slope of pasture, across
the stream, and over to the mountain that
reared above the village and gave it its name,
Unterberg. The summit was so high that he
could see it only by crouching, peering up as
far as he could. Even in summer, it was capped
in snow. Now it was late autumn, and the snow
swept down almost to the valley. The north face,
dark and sheer, was too steep for snow to cling
to. Even on the sunniest days it was bleak and
forbidding.

Its name, the Schritterhorn, made Tomas
think of jagged rocks, treacherous slopes and
shrieking winds. It was one of the highest
mountains in the Alps. For longer than anyone
could remember, mountaineers had come with
ropes and spikes and ice axes to climb it. Many
had failed. Many had died. The Schritterhorn
guarded its summit jealously – only the bravest
and most skilful were allowed to stand there.
And after that brief glory, they faced the
challenge of getting down.

'How sad,' people in the village would say,

when news of a death came. 'What a waste. What a pity.' And they would shake their heads and tut, and look at the mountain in reproach. But no one was really surprised.

Tomas was thinking about all those dead climbers. Wondering what they'd seen, and what had made them fall.

Downstairs, Mamma was boiling eggs for breakfast, looking for Johanna's mittens, hurrying Tomas to get ready for school. It was just like any ordinary weekday. But not ordinary at all.

Tomas felt himself sagging under the weight of this special, heavy day.

Winter, spring, summer and autumn had passed, and Pappi had missed it all. Everyone's birthday, his own birthday, Christmas . . .

There was such a big difference, Tomas thought, between 'nearly a year' and 'more than a year'. Would the time come when he and Mamma – Johanna, too, as she grew up – would say to each other, 'It's ten years ago today that Pappi left us'? And Johanna would barely remember.

Tomas had to say something, and his voice came out gruffly. 'It's the day. A year. A whole year.'

'Yes. Yes, it is.' Mamma hugged him.

'Does it mean he won't come back?'

'It's really only a day like any other day. Only one day since yesterday. No different, really.'

'It *seems* different, though.'

'I know. All we can do is keep hoping,' said Mamma, but something in her voice said that Hope had trickled away to nothing.

The eggs were ready to eat.

Tomas sat down, smashed the shell of his with a spoon, and swallowed a mouthful. It travelled painfully down his throat and lodged like a hard lump in his chest.

Trudging up the hill to school, Tomas saw Max, the carpenter, coming down the hill. Max's handcart was loaded with the stools and window boxes he was taking to Mamma.

As he drew near, Max called a cheery 'Good morning!' to Tomas. He often made deliveries at this time of day. Mamma would be getting Johanna ready to go to Nanni's house, and Max had taken to walking back up the lane with them, giving Johanna a ride on the handcart. She loved that. She would laugh and raise her arms to be lifted, just as she used to when she wanted Pappi to pick her up.

Tomas wasn't sure he liked Max being around so much, but Johanna clearly did. And – though he didn't like to think about it – so did Mamma. The sight of Max was enough to put a smile on her face, even when she was tired.

Karl was waiting outside the Alpenrose Inn.

'Come on! I've nearly turned into an icicle, waiting!'

He'd rolled snow into a ball while he waited, and they took turns kicking it up the street until it broke into pieces. Things began to seem more normal.

In the warmth of the schoolroom, Tomas opened his desk and saw a piece of paper inside. It was a crayoned drawing of a baggy black monster with horns like a bull, at the entrance to a cave. The monster stood tall, like a bear or a gorilla, and held a bone in one hand. Drops of blood dripped from its fangs, and more bones lay in a pile at its feet.

The writing, in wobbly capitals, said R.I.P. TOM'S DAD.

Tomas looked up. From his place at the front, Franz was glancing round, but when Tomas caught his eye he turned away and whispered to Peter. From Franz's smirk, Tomas knew the drawing was his.

Karl had seen. Tomas passed him the drawing, and he gave it a scornful glance.

'Stupid. Babyish. Can't even tell what it's meant to be.'

Tomas scrumpled it up in his hand and lobbed it at the back of Franz's head.

Fräulein Glockner was just coming in. 'Tomas Rust!' she snapped. 'We don't have that sort of behaviour, as you know very well! Pick that up at once and put it in the bin!'

The paper ball had bounced off Franz's head and fallen to the floor between the desks. As Tomas passed Franz and Peter, he heard a sneering laugh. He dropped the paper in the bin and made a show of wiping his hands on his jacket, as if he'd touched something slimy.

The drawing was all wrong, anyway, if it was meant to be the Brockenspectre. Pappi had never mentioned curling horns or pointy teeth. Franz's picture looked like something out of the picture books Johanna liked – a joke monster, not the slightest bit scary.

Nothing like the real Brockenspectre. The Brockenspectre that lived in Tomas's mind was all darkness and shadows.

'*RUAAAARGH!*' went Franz, at the end of school, as they collected their coats from the hooks outside the classroom. He made his hands into claws and showed his teeth in a snarl. Peter copied, laughing.

'Pathetic!' Tomas curled his hands into fists.

Karl pulled him away. 'Leave it, Tom. Not worth bothering with.'

As he followed Karl out, Tomas pretended not to hear the roaring noises and the laughter.

'He's only jealous,' Karl said. 'He'd give anything for a dad like yours.'

After a moment Tomas said, 'But so would I.' And he heard how sad and hopeless the words sounded.

At the school gate, the two pairs of boys turned in different directions. Peter and Franz both lived in the lane that wound downhill past the church, while Karl and Tomas went the other way, towards the Alpenrose. Tomas's cottage was farther along, where the village ended and the road began its downward slope to the valley.

As Tomas and Karl turned the bend, a pony trap wheeled round outside the inn, having left a large, bearded man at the door with several bags and cases. The pony looked at the boys through a bushy forelock, and steam rose from its flanks. It was a long pull up to the village from the railway station.

'You've got a new guest,' Tomas said to Karl,

as the man knocked on the inn's front door.

The driver clicked his tongue and the pony's iron-shod hooves rang on the metalled road as it clopped away.

'I'd better help with that luggage. See you tomorrow.' Karl hurried over to the newcomer.

Tomas felt restless as he walked home. He rather envied Karl. The inn was a cheerful place, its windows brightly lit throughout the dark evenings, its rooms full of laughter and talk, pipe-smoke and raised glasses, while the climbers talked of their adventures and made plans.

Mamma looked tired, as she kissed him and asked about his day at school. When he'd told her, he added, 'Someone was arriving at the inn. A big man with a beard and lots of bags.'

'That must be the new mountain guide,' Mamma said. 'Herr Donders has hired him for the winter.'

Yes, of course. Tomas had only glimpsed the man's weathered face and broad shoulders, but he should have guessed from the amount of baggage that he was here for more than a short stay.

At once Tomas disliked that man for not being Pappi, for taking his place. Everything seemed to be saying that Pappi wasn't coming back.

Chapter Six:

Man of the House

At break time next morning, Franz came up to
Tomas and Karl, suspiciously friendly.

'So you've met my uncle, then?' he said to Karl.

'Your uncle?' Tomas said sharply.

'The new guide. He's at the Alpenrose –
came yesterday. Philipp Goll. Onkel Philipp.
He's here for the whole winter. Didn't Karl tell
you?'

'No!' Tomas glanced at Karl, who looked uncomfortable.

'Well, you know now,' said Franz. 'I bet your father's pleased to get him, Karl. Onkel Philipp's the best there is. He knows his way around the mountains like no one else.'

'He'd need to,' said Karl, 'to be half as good as Tom's dad.'

Franz laughed loudly. 'Tom's dad!' he sneered. 'The famous Niklas Rust! What use was he, when he couldn't even save himself?'

Tomas's face went hot. 'You don't know that!'

'Oh? Where is he, then, your marvellous dad? Seen him lately, have you?'

'Come on, Tom.' Karl stepped between them, his back to Franz. 'I've got apple cake. Let's go outside.'

As soon as Franz was out of earshot, Tomas asked, 'Why didn't you say? About Franz's uncle?'

'I knew you wouldn't like it,' Karl said uneasily.

'Well, you were right. I don't.'

And when Karl offered him half the apple cake, Tomas shook his head and walked away.

Later, at home, he told Mamma the news.

'That new guide – it's Franz's uncle! Did you know? His name's Philipp Goll.'

'No!' Mamma was getting out her paints and brushes. 'I've seen him, though.'

'Franz keeps going on at me about Pappi,' Tomas told her.

'Does he? Well, your dad and Franz's didn't like each other. It goes back a long way. Now, weren't you going to clean out the chickens, and mend that broken bit of fence, and fetch more logs? It'll start to get dark soon.'

While he shovelled and swept and put down clean straw, Tomas kept thinking about

Franz's picture.

Although he knew it was nonsense, he couldn't stop wondering. Did Franz, perhaps, know something? If his uncle Philipp spent a lot of time in the mountains, maybe he really had come across a heap of bones by a cave. Tomas shivered.

But then, how could anyone tell whose bones they were?

When he'd finished his work, and shooed the clucking chickens into their house, he stood there for a moment, reluctant to go indoors. The marker day had been and gone, and his hope with it. Anyway, it had been the feeblest hope, no more substantial than the smoke wisping from the chimney. Today was just another day without Pappi.

When the air was clear, with no trace of mist or haze, you could look down the valley

towards the city and see the glimmer of lights across the lake. On still days you could hear the distant clatter of a train. Tomas stood on the brow of the meadow and looked down, feeling the hush of evening.

He thought of people down there in the city – smart city people. He thought of them going in and out of big buildings, eating meals in restaurants, going to the station to get on trains. Tomas had never been on a train. He imagined sitting in comfort while scenery flashed past, faster than a horse could gallop.

On the train, he'd heard, you could sit at a table while a waiter brought your dinner. You could sleep in a bedroom compartment, and when you woke up you'd be somewhere else. Even in another country.

Could Pappi have done that – bought a train ticket and gone away? But no – Pappi would never leave the mountains.

Tomas's nose, ears and fingers were getting cold, and he'd forgotten the logs. He collected a basketful from the woodshed.

Mamma gave him a grateful smile as he carried the logs in. 'You're such a big help, Tommi. I don't know what I'd do without you. You're the man of the house now.'

Sunday mornings were for church. Mamma always went, and although Tomas grumbled, he had to go too. So long sitting on a hard pew, while his mind wandered! He wanted to be outside.

Pappi never went to church. He just wouldn't, no matter how Mamma pleaded. She wanted to be like the other village women, walking to church arm-in-arm with her husband, just as Tomas now envied the children who had both father and mother with them. Some of them were in big family groups – like Karl, who had two lots of grandparents living in the village. Tomas only had Nanni. Grandpa had died three years ago, and there was no family at all on Pappi's side. He'd been alone until he met Mamma.

No matter how hard Mamma tried to persuade him, Pappi had no time for church, nor for all the chit-chat afterwards, when people lingered to talk before going home for their Sunday dinners.

'Everyone in this village wants to know everyone else's business,' he complained.

'Don't be like that! They're being friendly, not nosy,' Mamma would say.

Pappi wouldn't listen. 'I can't be doing with it.'

Today, as they entered, Tomas saw Max Oberlin in a pew near the front. He turned to give them all a beaming smile – or maybe it was just for Mamma.

During the prayers, Tomas gave her a sidelong look. Her lips were moving silently. He wondered if she still prayed for Pappi to return.

Tomas thought about being called the man of the house. It made him uneasy. A little bit proud, yes, and important. But he didn't feel ready to be a man. Pappi was the *man of the house*, not him.

As people spilled out into the churchyard, Tomas went over to Karl, wanting to make up for yesterday.

'Let's go out later with your sledge! There's good snow on the slopes above our field.'

Karl looked uneasy. 'That'd be fun, but I've promised to go walking with Philipp. Show him some of the paths.'

Tomas kicked at a loose stone. 'Philipp? You mean Franz's Onkel Philipp?'

Karl nodded.

'I thought he knew everything about the mountains already? That's what Franz says.'

'He knows the high routes,' Karl said. 'He

doesn't know the paths that lead up from here.'

'Can't he read a map?'

'Don't be huffy, Tom. You could come, too. It'll be fun. Anyway, Philipp's all right. It's not his fault he's Franz's uncle.'

'Is Franz going?'

'Well – I don't think so.'

'But you're not sure.' Tomas turned away. 'No. You go if you want. I'm not coming.'

After church, Mamma, Tomas and Johanna always had Sunday dinner at Nanni's house. Today when the meal was over Tomas felt too fidgety to stay indoors. When they'd finished, he told Mamma that he was meeting Karl and Philipp Goll. Instead, though, he set off by himself.

He felt uneasy, lying, but he was so restless that he had to do *some*thing.

He took the route he had taken with Pappi, up the bouldery path that climbed beside the Schneegletscher. Just above the village, the glacier dwindled into a trickle of meltwater, but the higher he climbed, the thicker and icier it was. Cold air rose from it, chilling his face.

Maybe Karl and Philipp Goll would come this way, and Franz. If he met them, he'd say a cool hello, and walk on past.

But no one was around. He looked up towards the Schritterhorn summit. The air smelled of pine, and low sunlight slanted through the trees.

He stood by the edge of the ice river, choppy as a rough sea, dirty white at the edges, with blue in its crevices and folds. Its coldness hung in the air like a spell.

He remembered Pappi's warning. *You might think it looks solid,* said Pappi's voice in his head, *but you mustn't walk on it. You could fall in and never get out.*

Tomas was in the sort of mood that made him want to try.

He stepped onto the ice and stood on a frozen curl, feeling its unevenness. Stretching out a foot, he balanced on a loose chunk. His next foothold began to give way, with a splitting and a creaking that made him step back hastily.

He couldn't tell how thick the ice was, even here at the edges.

The glacier didn't care. He was nothing to it, smaller than a fly on a cow's flank. It could swallow him alive. It would continue its slow, centuries-old descent, and no one would know. He would disappear into the cold, crushing depths.

No. He wasn't going to be one of those bodies found frozen in ice.

Could that be what had happened to Pappi? In spite of all his knowledge, all his mountain-craft, all his lack of fear, had something made him try to cross a glacier – high in the mountain, above the tree line, where no one had found him? In years to come, as the ice slid slowly downwards, would someone come across an arm or a leg poking through the surface, and find Pappi – a frozen statue of a man?

It was a horrible thought. Tomas pushed it away, and headed back to the village.

Glacier

Wide frozen river. Slow, slow glide.

Rain and snow from winters past, held in seeming stillness.

But not.

Wait. Listen.

Listen. Wait.

The creak and scritch of the valleywards slide. Stones and bones tumbled and polished. Chasms open, chunks form.

Blue of caught sky tricks the eye.

Can water carve rock? Can ice cut through mountains, shape valleys?

Yes, in the slowness of time. In earth-time, that measures the shaping of continents, the forming of moons and planets, the birth of stars.

Time moves slowly.

Time moves quickly.

Life flows in an instant, but the frozen river is old as the mountains' making.

Chapter Seven:

Johanna's Bedtime Story

'You're back early!' said Mamma. 'Didn't you go far?'

'Not really. And we walked quickly.'

'And what was Herr Goll like?'

'He was . . . all right.' Tomas bent down to unlace his boots, avoiding Mamma's eye. She could often tell when he was hiding something.

'Don't take your boots off, Tommi – I want

you to take six eggs round to Frau Kümmel.
I promised them to her after church. Then,
if you give Johanna her tea, and heat up the
water for her bath, I'll get on with these window
boxes.'

Tomas sighed. There were always jobs waiting
for him. Perhaps that was what Mamma meant
by *the man of the house*.

Later, when Johanna was ready for bed, he
carried her up the ladder to her cot in the attic
bedroom. She smelled sweet and warm from
her bath. She was growing fast, and was almost
too big for her cot. Soon she would need a
proper bed. Max was making one, and Mamma
was going to paint it in time for Christmas.

Johanna wouldn't lie down, but stood up
against the bars of the cot, grabbing Tomas's
arm. 'Story! Story!'

Usually Tomas liked making up stories for
Johanna, and sometimes songs. She liked to
hear the same ones over and over again. Her
favourite was about a dog who wouldn't go out
in the snow until his owner knitted two pairs of

boots for him. Today, though, when she settled down, sucking her thumb and looking at him, something made him start a new story.

'Once upon a time there was a mountain monster. A big, shadowy monster who lived by himself in a cave – high, high up in the craggiest tops. Only a few people ever saw him, and those who did would never forget it. For ever after, he followed them in their dreams.'

Johanna's eyes were big and round, watching his face.

'He's the biggest monster you ever saw. A giant of a monster. A huge black shadow. He walks behind you through the trees. When you turn round he hides behind the rocks. You won't see him unless he wants you to. And you'll never get away. If you run, he'll be there, too. He won't let you go.'

The story wanted him to carry on, even though he saw the dismay in Johanna's face.

'And when he decides, he'll grab you with his gnarly hands and drag you to his cave, and eat you all up till there's nothing left but bones, and a few rags of clothes.'

Johanna's mouth opened wide and went square. There was a moment of silence while her lungs filled with air. Then she let out a scream. It was a scream Tomas had never heard before, unbelievably loud for such a small person – a scream that brought Mamma racing up the ladder.

'Jo! Tommi! Whatever's happened?'

What had he done? Why hadn't he told Johanna one of the simple, happy stories she liked? Had he *wanted* to frighten her?

He backed off, getting out of Mamma's way, as she lifted Johanna out of the cot and clasped her tightly.

'Shh, shh, little darling! What happened?' she asked Tomas. 'Did she fall? Has she hurt herself?'

'No.' Tomas's voice came out sulkily. 'I was just telling her a story.'

'*Don't* eat me! *Don't* eat me!' Johanna could hardly get the words out – she was shaking with sobs. 'Monster go 'way!'

'Shh! Shh! There isn't a monster, darling. Tommi, what have you been telling her?'

'Just a story I made up.'

'A scary monster story? Haven't you got more sense? Do you want to give her nightmares? Shh, shh, little precious. Everything's all right – there's no monster. Tommi didn't mean it. He'll tell you a nice story now.'

'No,' Tomas grumped. 'I don't want to.'

He clomped down the ladder and sat at the table, staring into the fire, chin propped on hands.

Little precious. Little darling. It was all Johanna, wasn't it? He heard the soothing voice Mamma used for Johanna, and the grating crossness of her words to *him*.

He scowled and brooded until Mamma came down, saying that Johanna was asleep at last. She asked Tomas if he'd help with the painting.

'Do I have to?'

'No, Tomas, you don't,' said Mamma, in a tight, careful way.

She started work, mixing her colours, while he watched. He felt even worse now. If she'd said yes, he *did* have to, he could have argued back.

After a moment he snatched up a brush.

His job was to paint the background colour of the stools, chairs and window boxes, ready for Mamma to do the skilled work of flowers or scenery. He dipped his brush into yellow paint.

'Did something go wrong this afternoon?' Mamma asked him. 'When you were with Karl and Herr Goll?'

Tomas shook his head and bent over his work.

An idea slipped into his mind – a stupid, senseless, irresistible idea.

Chapter Eight:

The Son of Niklas Rust

It was a crazy idea, he knew. But one that wouldn't go away.

Why not go into the mountains to look for Pappi?

And what was the use of just thinking about it?

These last few days, the weather had been

good – bright, cold autumn sunshine, with clear skies. If he waited any longer, winter would be here, and the snows would come, and it would be too late.

I'm the son of Niklas Rust, he told himself, *and I'm going to prove it. Niklas Rust wouldn't sit at home waiting. He'd go out and do something. And so will I.*

And the way of doing it shaped itself while he worked the paint to and fro along the sides of the window box.

If he put a few things into a rucksack . . . tonight, very quietly, after Mamma had gone to bed . . . No. Tomorrow night would be better. He needed time for proper planning. An expedition must be prepared for. He knew that, from Pappi.

So, tomorrow night. Then, on Tuesday, if he pretended to go to school as usual . . .

If, after he'd kissed Mamma goodbye and she watched him go up the street, he doubled back along the stream below the field and went round behind the woodshed . . .

If he waited till she'd gone up the hill with Johanna, to Nanni's house . . .

Then he could collect his rucksack and go.

He knew where he'd head for. He'd go all the way up to the high pass used by travellers to cross to the other side of the mountain range. There was a monastery up there, and if he continued along the ridge he'd come to the remote mountain huts where Pappi had liked to sleep. He couldn't climb the high peaks by himself without ropes and an ice axe – certainly not the Schritterhorn – but the ridge was where he was most likely to meet other walkers. People who had climbed up from other towns and villages – people who might have seen Pappi, or know where he was.

There were dangers up there. Of course there were. There might even be the Brockenspectre, waiting for him, knowing he'd come. At the thought, he felt the icy slither of fear down his back. But if he didn't face those risks he'd be angry with himself for staying at home, doing nothing. Never knowing any more than he knew now.

He'd leave a note for Mamma, explaining – he couldn't let her think he'd just disappeared. She'd be cross, of course, but he'd face that when he got back.

And if he *did* find Pappi, she'd be so delighted that she wouldn't be cross at all.

Mamma was still cool with him in the morning. He knew that it was only partly for frightening Johanna – more because he hadn't said sorry. He *was* sorry, especially now that his bad mood was replaced by secret excitement, but he didn't dare say so for fear of giving too much away.

It was Mamma he was sorry for now, knowing how awful she'd feel when she found his note. She'd think it was because she'd told him off. But his plan had taken hold of him – he couldn't change his mind now.

Karl was waiting outside the Alpenrose.

'You should have come yesterday! It was just Philipp and me – no Franz. We had a good walk.'

'Didn't matter. I went up to the glacier by myself.'

'That was silly! You know the first rule of the mountains – never go on your own.'

Tomas shrugged. 'My dad did, all the time.'

'Yes,' said Karl, 'and you're just like him. Obstinate.'

Tomas felt an inner glow at being compared to his father. For a moment he thought of telling Karl his plan, but stopped in time. Karl would think it was a crazy idea. He might tell his father, or Philipp Goll.

'Philipp's first group is arriving this week,' Karl told him. 'He's asked me to walk with them on Saturday. Why don't you come too?'

'Maybe.'

Saturday, Tomas thought. *Five whole days away!* What would have happened by then? Where would he be? He couldn't think so far ahead. Everything would look different by Saturday.

That evening, when it was Johanna's bedtime and Mamma was busy telling her a story and singing a song, Tomas took bread and cheese and apples from the larder, hoping Mamma wouldn't notice they were missing. He filled a bottle with water, and put these things in his small rucksack, along with a warm sweater, a spare pair of socks, and one of Pappi's old maps.

Up in the attic he wrote a note, and hid it under his pillow to leave out in the morning.

Dear Mamma,

Please don't worry. I have gone to look for Pappi. I might be gone for a few days. See you soon.

Love from Tommi

It felt final now. He could hardly sleep – his head was so full of excitement and worry.

He was no longer sure that his plan was such a good one. All the dangers of the mountains crowded into his mind – crevasses, rock falls, avalanches, maybe even wolves. And that was without even thinking of the mountain spirits people talked about – the voices that wailed from the summits, the cacklers who hurled stones at unwary travellers, and the nameless, fearsome creatures that roamed the high places.

And the Brockenspectre – waiting, waiting . . .

But I can't not go, Tomas thought. *Not when I've got this far.*

If he gave up now, before he'd even started, he'd feel like a coward.

He wasn't a coward. He was his father's son. And everyone knew how brave his father was.

'I am the son of Niklas Rust,' Tomas whispered to himself, to chase away his fears.

PART THREE

Mountain

Come, and I will be part of you.

Come once to my heights, and you will return.

I will enter your spirit and haunt you for ever.

My sublime beauty will lure you, keep you, change you.

Though you fear me, you must come. Lowlands and flatlands will never charm you. Always your soul will yearn for mountains.

You know my dangers, and must respect them.

Observe my creatures, those that live with me and do not fear.

You must be fearful. You are human.

I offer no protection.

You cannot fly with the eagle, leap with the chamois, or starve with the wolf while you wait for prey.

You are two-footed, clumsy and slow.

Still you come. You flounder in snow. Gulp the

thin air. Quail at the rumble of stonefall.

Never will you escape my spell.
  Never will you wish to.

Chapter Nine:

Busy Bustlers, Sleeping Dog

Waking up, Tomas half hoped that the weather had turned stormy or foggy, giving him a reason not to go. But he opened his curtains and saw that the sky was already lightening, the stars fading. There was no wind. The Schritterhorn was emerging from darkness to loom over the village.

He ate a bigger breakfast than usual. Saying goodbye to Mamma and Johanna, he tried to sound as if it was a normal school day, and he'd be home by tea time.

Following his plan, he crept back to the cottage, hid behind the woodshed and waited. Soon he heard Mamma locking the door, and talking to Johanna as they walked up the street towards Nanni's house, hand in hand.

He had to take a winding way out of the village – he couldn't walk past the inn and the church, or people would see him. A footpath led down to the stream below the cottage, over a bridge, and up through the woods below the Schritterhorn to the foot of the glacier.

In the woods he stopped and looked back. There was no changing his mind now. He was on his way to find Pappi.

Tomas climbed steadily for more than an hour, up the bouldery path beside the glacier. He reached the ice-covered tarn and paused to drink from his bottle. The village was out of view, hidden by trees and a rocky outcrop. He could see only the church spire, and sunlit fir trees on the far side of the valley.

He put his bottle away and carried on climbing. He felt free – the day was his own. He'd decide how far to go, and when to stop and rest. Karl, and the others at school, would think he was ill, and had stayed at home. He wondered what they were doing: arithmetic, maybe, or a spelling test.

Soon he was making his way through the last of the silver birches and dwarf pines, and up into the snow. It was colder here, and he stopped to take his scarf and gloves out of his rucksack. His boots crunched on fresh snow, and the low sun dazzled.

Once he stopped to look at the map. His path would take him to the top of the pass, and the monastery. He should reach it by dusk.

He was panting as he climbed the steep path, reaching for handholds. Whichever way he looked now, there were only mountains – peaks and slopes as far as his eyes could reach. He felt tiny, a small dot of a boy in the vast landscape. And proud, because he'd come here alone.

The farther he went, the farther he'd have to walk back. He'd rarely climbed as high as this, and always Pappi had been with him, leading the way. Even so, there were times when the only way to keep going had been to take one step, then another, and not think of the distance still to go.

There had been times when the bitter wind drummed his ears and beat his brain into confusion. There had been times when he thought that if only he could get home safely, he'd never go near a mountain again.

But all those times, Pappi had been there.
Now . . . Never in his life had Tomas felt so
alone.

Pappi hadn't minded being lonely. He liked
it. He sought out loneliness.

You must always keep your head, said Pappi's
voice. *When things go wrong, you mustn't panic.
Panic, and you'll make stupid mistakes.*

Thinking of Pappi was a way of not feeling
alone. But *one mistake* . . . That thought lodged
in his mind and wouldn't go away. Had Pappi,
even Pappi, made a bad mistake? Taken a false
step that had been his last? And why – had
something startled him into faltering?

Tomas felt the prickle of fear at the back of
his neck.

To his right, the Schritterhorn bulked against
the sky, craggy and vast. Tomas thought of the
people who'd lost their lives trying to reach the
summit. They had pitted themselves against the
mountain, and had lost.

Tomas was so used to seeing the mass of

the Schritterhorn behind the village
that he looked on it as a stern
guardian. From here, closer, he
saw the steepness of its slopes
and the darkness of its crags
and screes. He shivered.

It was too cold to stand still.
He tugged his collar up, his
cap down, and his scarf
more tightly around his
neck, and walked on.

A shrill chittering made him
look up. He expected to see a
bird – a raven or maybe an eagle –
but instead, on the curve of the hill, he
saw a fat furry creature that stood up to look
at him. Against the snow it was red-grey, with a
paler face. It was like a squirrel, the biggest and
fattest squirrel ever seen, but Tomas knew it was
a marmot. They were a common enough sight
on high ground. He'd come across a few of
them on his walks with Pappi.

The marmot repeated its chattering call – so loud that it seemed to echo off the slopes. A second one scampered over the snow to join it. They stood up to each other, sparring like boxers, then started to play-fight. As they rolled down the slope they snuffled and grunted, yipped and yapped.

Tomas couldn't help laughing.

The sound made the marmots stop their play and turn to stare, noses waffling. Then, whisking their tails, they were off, bounding behind rocks and out of view.

They had a burrow nearby, he guessed. The settled weather had brought them out to look for food.

He always liked to see marmots – so plump, so cheerful in their busy bustling.

As he carried on climbing he wondered what the time was. It must surely be well past midday, and the light would soon fade. He stopped in the shelter of an overhang to eat a little of his bread and cheese. But sitting made him cold, and he had to save most of his food for later. He'd need to make haste, to reach the monastery by dusk.

He walked on steadily, banging his arms against his sides to bring life back to his hands.

The light was changing. Before long he could only dimly see the path ahead. Mist crept silently, and snow was starting to fall. It was hard to tell how much daylight was left.

Would the monks let him in? What if the doors were bolted and the shutters closed?

There was still a little grey light left when he saw the walls looming ahead. The bleak stone building stood at the top of the pass, exposed to wind and blizzards.

Relief rushed through him. There would be food here, and warmth.

He worked his way round the wall to the iron gates and was letting himself through into the courtyard when he realized how silly he'd been. He couldn't stay the night at the monastery like any grown-up person, then carry on tomorrow. If he knocked on the door and asked for shelter, the monks would never let him set off again on his own. A young boy, alone in the mountains!

It was foolish, and he knew it, and so would they. They'd want him to stay with them, or they'd arrange for someone to take him back to Unterberg, and safety.

Then – he'd find nothing. Prove nothing. He'd be taken home like a little lost boy.

He couldn't give himself over to them; he couldn't give up his plan.

What, then? He was ready to sink to the ground with weariness, to sleep and sleep. There must be some kind of shed or outbuilding where he could shelter for the night without the monks knowing.

The lamplight at the windows tempted him. He imagined the monks preparing their meal, eating together, warmed by a fire of glowing logs. He weakened at the thought. But he didn't go up to the big main door. Instead he went over to a cluster of low buildings to one side.

A smell of warm straw reached him. Did the

monks keep cows here, or even a horse? He saw a door divided in two, like a stable. Carefully he unbolted the top half and eased it open.

From inside, he heard a low growl, and then a *whuff*. He heard the sound of an animal getting to its feet – not hooves, but a soft padding as the creature came close to him. A huge head loomed, and his face was warmed by dog breath. A rough tongue licked his hand.

The mountain dog! Of course – he knew that the monks kept a dog to help with rescues. Pappi had helped in searches where this dog had led the way. Once Tomas had seen the dog for himself, when a search party came down beside the

Schneegletscher to the village. His name was Bruno, Pappi had said, and he was a kindly old thing.

Tomas hoped so! Carefully he opened the lower door – just enough to sidle through. The earth floor was strewn with straw. The dog had got up from his bed, a heap of stuffed sacks in one corner.

'Bruno! Good boy!' Tomas whispered.

In the gloom of the stable Tomas saw the wide brown-and-white face that seemed to smile at him. Bruno was a heavy dog, the size of a small pony, with a thick furry coat.

This would be a good place to spend the night. He'd be safe and snug with the big dog to warm him.

'Lie down, Bruno.' Tomas latched his fingers underneath the dog's sturdy collar, and guided him towards the sacking bed.

Bruno seemed pleased to have company. He lay down again with a contented grunt. Tomas took off his boots, and lay curled against him.

Chapter Ten:
Sleepwalking

Tomas slept soundly, but woke early when the dog stirred beside him.

He took a few moments to remember where he was.

Getting to his feet, he carefully opened the top half of the stable door, and peered out. It was dark, but he saw lamplight through the high monastery windows, moving slowly along and out of view. He knew from Pappi that the monks got up very early, for prayers in the chapel.

What time would they come to feed Bruno and let him out? Tomas was suddenly fearful. He mustn't be found!

He pulled on his boots and fastened his rucksack. He didn't want to leave Bruno, his warm and comforting friend, but he couldn't risk waiting for daylight.

He threw his arms around the dog's neck.

'Goodbye, Bruno! Thank you. Maybe I'll see you on my way back.'

Outside the monastery gates, he felt more alone than ever. If only Bruno could have come with him! Things would seem so different with a dog companion.

It was too dark to see his way clearly, but the first paleness of dawn was showing in the east. Tomas sheltered by a rock, shivering, to eat his breakfast, then went on his way as the sky lightened.

There was no risk of getting lost. The path

from the monastery was well-used, the snow trodden down between banks. It led along the ridge and into the heart of the mountain range. Along it, he would come to several refuge huts, and with luck he'd meet someone coming the other way – someone who'd seen Pappi, or had news. Sometimes, Pappi said, people left messages in the huts – scraps of paper pinned to a wall or nailed to the inside of the door.

The sun spilled gold as it rose above the summits. Tomas's shadow walked alongside him, rippling over the wind-crusted snow. There was even a faint warmth. For the first hour or two he felt full of energy, as if he could walk all day. He was Niklas Rust's son, after all – it was in his blood.

And it was so beautiful here that he knew deep inside himself why Pappi loved the mountains. The ordinary world of village and school seemed far, far away. He was above it all, looking down over an expanse of snow and forest. He saw cold blue slopes on the northern faces, and an ice-field gleaming golden in sunlight. In the heights he saw needle-like pinnacles where only ravens and eagles would perch, or the chamois, the sure-footed mountain goats that seemed fearless even at the most dizzying heights. To his right, the Schritterhorn was hiding its sheer, terrible drop, showing him only the gentle rise of its southern slopes. If he didn't know better he might have thought it an easy stroll from here to its summit.

Farther on, the ridge

narrowed, and now the ground dropped steeply away on either side. Before long he should reach the first of the mountain huts.

He was walking into mist.

Tomas had spent enough time on the mountain slopes to have seen all kinds of weather: sunny days, hot enough to burnish his face, but also lashing hail, dizzying blizzards, and gales that threatened to blow him off his feet.

Don't ever take the weather for granted, boy, said Pappi. *That's how people get themselves stuck, or lost. It might be warm and sunny down in the valley, but mountains make their own weather. A fine day can change to storm. Light rain can turn to hailstones. A little breeze can whip up into a frenzy. You must be prepared for everything.*

It was harder now to put one foot in front of the other. He was tiring. His legs felt heavy, his mind dull. He couldn't be sure he was still on the track. At first he'd been walking on firm-packed snow, but now he was sinking into drifts up to his knees.

As the mist thickened, it blurred his eyes

and clammed his lashes. He was confused by the whiteness of snow, whiteness of mist. He had only his sense of direction to guide him, and how trustworthy was that? His hands were numb, and he curled them into fists inside his gloves.

He was chilled with fear. It iced his limbs and clutched at his breath.

Why had he come?

If he didn't find a mountain hut, if he wandered away from the track . . . what then? His only shelter would be a place below rocks, or maybe in a cave.

A cave. But there he might find the Brockenspectre. Or the Brockenspectre might find him.

He'd imagined it often enough, seen himself blundering through the white blindness, with no idea which way to go . . . and the shadowy terror would be waiting.

What if he saw it now? Where would he run to? Even if he *could* run, with snow clogging his steps . . .

This was madness.

In his mind, Pappi said, *Don't panic. You must never panic.*

He had two choices: either turn back to the monastery . . . or keep going.

Surely, though, the hut couldn't be far ahead. And it was a long way back to the pass. The only thing to do was keep trudging on.

One step, another.

One step, another.

From time to time the dark shape of a rock loomed into view, and he brushed moisture from his lashes, trying to see clearly.

A pleasant warmth began to seep through him. He was walking in a dreamy, almost sleepy way, and nothing seemed very important.

Perhaps he'd sit down and rest.

He knew he shouldn't. People died like that, in the mountains – numbed into stupidity, snow-dazed. Pappi's voice was saying, *No, no! Sit down and you'll never get up again . . .*

But he was too tired to listen, and the voice came from a long, long way off.

What – uh – whoa—

He was slipping, sliding . . .

Lurching, toppling . . .

His left foot waved in empty air as the snow gave way with a soft slither. He glimpsed the dark shapes of trees in mist, a long way below.

He flung himself at the slope and grabbed for holds with both hands, finding none. He was a human sledge, hurtling fast down the slope. Ice crystals burned his face. Faster and faster he slid.

He would die.

He was as good as dead.

At any moment he would slam into rocks and lie there, broken . . .

Then the crack and crash of branches, snagging his rucksack, turning him the wrong way up, scratching his face.

And a dizzy stillness. His head

whirled with the suddenness of stopping. Slowly his eyes made out a muddle of twigs and snow and sky. His heart was pounding.

A low tree had caught him. Ended his fall. Saved him.

He was alive, gasping. Apart from jarred legs and thorn-scratched face, he was unhurt. His mind flooded with thanks.

When he'd stopped trembling, he untangled the straps of his rucksack from the branches, and lowered himself into deep snow. Then he looked up to see how far he'd fallen.

His landing spot was a thicket of low, thorny trees huddled against the hillside. He was lucky – luckier than he deserved.

He'd let himself be lulled by the mist and the cold. He'd stopped thinking, and that could have been the last mistake he ever made. Half asleep, he'd strayed into a cornice – snow that had built up in a crack between rocks, snow supported by nothing. Snow that had slid away as he stepped into it.

Pappi had told him that climbers were killed

like that every year – thinking there was solid rock underneath, finding nothing but snow, falling to their deaths. Many a time Pappi had spoken of the dangers of cornices, and the importance of staying alert.

Only a fool goes into the mountains unprepared, said Pappi. *Only a fool takes risks.*

And the biggest risk of all was to set out alone, without telling anyone where he was going. He'd broken the most basic rule, doing that.

Take risks in the mountains and you deserve to die, said Pappi.

I do *deserve it, then,* thought Tomas.

But he was going to try his hardest to survive.

He was the son of Niklas Rust.

Chapter Eleven:
Hut

The first thing was to get his bearings, and work out what to do.

One thing was for sure – he couldn't go back up the way he'd come down. The cliff above him was almost sheer above the trees, with no footholds. No one could climb that without ropes and an ice axe.

To reach the hut and – eventually – return

home, he'd have to regain the ridge somehow. The only thing to do was work his way along the tree line, looking for a way up.

The forest he was in was low and dense. Thorny trees clung to the hillside, wind-battered, leaning into the slope. A crow cawed, lifted itself on spread wings and flew away.

He lost track of time as he walked. Hours must have passed, and he had no hope now of getting up to the ridge before nightfall. He'd have to shelter in the trees. He should have turned back for the monastery while he had the chance.

The plashing of water made him stop to listen. It wasn't far ahead. The sound grew louder as he approached, and soon he found himself standing below a high waterfall. Mist rose like steam where a column of water crashed down to rocks, pooling in a small tarn. At the lower end, water funnelled into a glassy slide between rocks, then ran fast downhill through snow banks and stands of trees.

Chunks and splinters of rock showed that

part of the cliff above had crumbled away.
Icicles speared down from an overhang. Tomas
thought about climbing, but saw that it would
be impossible. Clambering over the slippery,
ice-glazed crags – even if he could do it – could
easily start a new rock fall.

He drank, filled his water bottle from the
torrent, and ate some of his bread and cheese,
worried now that he had only a few morsels left.
Then, shouldering his rucksack, he continued
on his way.

All along he'd tried to stay above the forest,
but now a high wall of rock gave him no choice
but to find a path through the trees.

The snow lay thinly here. Although thorns
clutched at his clothes and hair he had the
feeling that he was on a track, and that others
had walked this way.

Reaching a small clearing, open to the sky,
he saw a simple wooden cross planted in the
ground. He saw a hummock under the snow
where small boulders had been piled. A sprig of
scarlet berries lay at the foot of the cross.

A grave.

It was a strange place to find one, far from the nearest village or church. He walked closer, and brushed off the snow that clung to the crosspiece. He thought there might be a carved name, but there was nothing.

Who had been here? Had a group of mountaineers buried a dead companion? Someone had fallen from the ridge, perhaps – or had died of exposure?

The thought chilled him.

Then he noticed something else.

Footprints! The snow
around the grave was
trampled. A line of footprints
led to the spot, and back
the way they'd come, in the
direction he was heading.

He blinked. Stared. Stooped
to examine the prints more
closely, and touch them.

His first thought was that
they could be the prints of
Pappi's boots. But they were no
larger than his own, not big
enough for Pappi. And a trail
of paw-prints ran along beside.

Whoever had left those

prints had a dog with them. It couldn't have been long ago, or the prints would have been filled with new snow. That same person must have left the sprig of berries.

Tomas followed the tracks. They soon joined a well-trodden path through the trees. His pace quickened. After the loneliness of the last two days, at last he'd meet someone. He hoped they'd be friendly.

He heard barking. Out of the trees came a black-and-white shape, bounding joyfully towards him.

'Here, dog! Good dog!' Tomas called.

The smiley-faced dog dashed in circles around him. Then it ran ahead, turning to see if he was coming.

The path of trodden snow led to another small clearing by the cliff-face.

Tomas blinked and stared, not quite believing what he saw. Built against the rock was a hut, with stone walls, a wooden door, and lamplight through a curtained window.

Was he dreaming?

The door opened, and a voice called, 'Fritzi! Fritzi! Is someone there?'

It was an old woman. Silver-haired, older than Nanni, well wrapped up in layers of cloth and knitted wool.

'Who is it?' she called, and stared at Tomas with weak, watery eyes.

'My name's Tomas.'

'Why, you're just a boy!' she said, as he walked closer. 'Come on in – you look half frozen!'

Inside the hut, Tomas looked around in astonishment.

He had stepped out of the world of ice and snow into one of warmth and lamplight. A log smouldered in the hearth, and a lamp

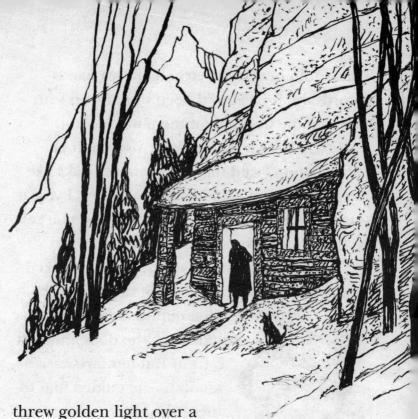

threw golden light over a
rocking chair and a rag rug.
Something was cooking in a pot hung above the
fire – something deliciously meaty and herby.
The dog settled down on the rug.

'What, are you on your own, boy?' asked the
old woman. 'Lost? You're young to be out on
your own.'

'I . . . was heading for the mountain hut,'

Tomas told her. He stretched out his hands towards the fire. They'd been so numbed with cold that the warming of them was painful.

'Well, you're a long way off. You won't get there tonight,' said the old woman. 'Looks like you need a good feed and a good sleep. I've got some ointment for those scratches. And you're lucky – I've made rabbit broth today.'

Tomas was starting to wonder if he'd walked out of a dream and into a fairy tale. Might the welcoming old woman turn into a witch? Slam the door and bolt it firm? But her face was kindly as she guided him to the single chair.

'Where are you from, then? What's brought you here alone?' she asked, as she smeared herb-scented ointment on his face.

'Don't mind me being nosy, boy. I don't get many visitors. It's usually just me and Fritzi.'

She ladled broth into a bowl for him and he ate it hungrily, answering her questions between mouthfuls. After that it was tempting to nod off to sleep. But he had questions of his own – questions that were, after all, the whole point of his journey.

'Have you seen—' he began.

At the same moment, the old woman spoke, too. 'You know, you remind me of my son. That's him, back there.'

Tomas looked at the wall above the hearth, expecting to see a photograph. But the old woman was pointing beyond the wall of the cottage, out and beyond.

'You must have passed the grave? The mound? That's him. That's my son.'

Old Woman

Yes. My boy. My only son.

He was killed in a rock fall, climbing the ravine. Now he'll stay there.

Oh yes. Awful.

I never saw much of him, though. He came once or twice a year. About this time, before winter set in, he'd bring me oil for the lamps, and matches, and a few other things, and then off he'd go.

Never stayed long. Didn't have much time for his old mother.

Fifteen years I've been living here like a hermit. Maybe more. I lose track of time. Built this hut myself – I was younger and stronger then. That was after my husband died, and my son grew up and left home.

Now there's just me and Fritzi. We don't need much. We've got water from the spring, and the freshest air you could wish for, and the mountains for our garden. That's all I want. I'll stay here till I die. Fritzi's my eyes and ears, these days.

My son's the same. Lives for the mountains. Used to, I mean.

What happened? Well, the weather was foul, the day he came. And next morning. He'd stayed the night and he was keen to be off, no matter what.

His plan was to climb up the gorge there. If he'd walked ten miles farther along the cliff he'd have found an easy track up, but he was a climber and he was big and strong and he had to do things his own way.

It wasn't a day to go out if you didn't have to. I'd have stayed in, but I needed more wood. So I got my sledge, and Fritzi and I walked with him as far as the clearing. Then we said goodbye and off he went.

I was on my way back with the wood when I heard the rock fall.

I found him dead by the tarn. My boy. So big and strong. All the life crushed out of him. Oh, I wept and I wailed for a bit. He wasn't kind to me, but he was my son all the same. The only one I had.

After a while, I fetched my shovel and started digging in the clearing there. Oh, it was hard work! With all the rocks and tree roots I needed an axe as well. Took me two whole days of blisters and stiff arms. Had to do it, though. The last thing I'd ever do for my boy.

When I couldn't dig any more I heaved him onto the sledge and I gave him the best burial I could. I said a prayer or two and I even sang a hymn. It's not a churchyard but he's in the mountains, and that's better. If this isn't God's garden then I don't know what is.

Where was he off to? Well, boy, he'd come to say goodbye. He was off on a long journey. Heading all the way over the Alps to Italy, he said, to that north part of Italy high in the mountains.

When he got there he'd stay, he said. Make a new life for himself. He'd had enough of his old one. He had a wife and two children, but he'd left them behind. I told him that was wrong, but there was no stopping him once he'd made his mind up.

Oh yes, he had a family. Down in Unterberg.

Are you all right, boy? You look pale. Come on, shift a bit nearer to the fire.

I never met them. He didn't want me in his life, or theirs. I don't think he wanted anyone.

Shouldn't have married, if you ask me. Too fond of his own way. I can't see him as a good husband, or a good father.

What are you staring at? Oh, that painted bird? That was his. He had it with him, that last time. I found it on the floor where he slept.

After he'd gone I put it up on the shelf to keep. It's the only thing I've got of his.

So he's here now, my Niklas, just a step away. I go there every day with flowers in summer or berries in winter. He's with me more than he ever was in his life.

I'll put another log on. You look chilled to the bone, boy.

PART FOUR

Chapter Twelve:

Rant

Tomas couldn't sleep.

He lay under rough blankets on a sack stuffed with straw. The fire was smouldering, and Fritzi lay as close to it as he could get. The old woman snored gently in her own sack bed.

Although Tomas's limbs ached with tiredness, his mind was spinning.

He kept going over and over everything the

old woman had said. He had both found and lost his father in her words.

His father was dead, lying in a stony grave.

But if he hadn't died, he would have been lost to the family anyway, by his own choice.

Pappi, Pappi – how could you leave us? How could you walk out of the door and never mean to come back?

But he had. He had wanted to leave them behind. Wanted never to see them again. And a worse thought came to Tomas –

Was it me? What I said? Is it all my fault?

And . . . the old woman. She was –

He couldn't properly take it in, but she was his *grandmother*. A second grandmother, hidden from him all his life. He had *always* had two grandmothers, and not known.

Pappi had lied about that – he'd always said that he had no other family. Tomas turned over, and turned again, unable to get comfortable, unable to stop his mind from whirling.

When I see Pappi, I'll tell him how unfair he's

been, Tomas thought – then: *But – no. I never will.*

Never. Never see Pappi again.

Never.

It seemed too short and simple a word to hold so terrible a meaning.

At last he drifted into sleep.

He dreamed that he was lost in the mountains, in the white blindness. He was on the brink of a giddy drop, looking for a way down. Darkness covered him, the shadow of a huge figure that towered above. It was so tall that his eyes had to travel up it, peering to the very top. Still he couldn't see its face.

He knew it was the Brockenspectre.

It moved closer. For a moment he thought it would kick or push him over the edge. He raised his arms and tried to skitter out of reach, floundering in snow.

The Brockenspectre tilted its head to stare down at him. Its look was scornful. It didn't kick or push – didn't touch him at all. But that gaze of contempt was worse.

The face was his father's.

'Did you think I'd be with you for ever?' it said.

Then it turned and walked away, fading into the mist.

Waking up, he felt heavy and dull, remembering where he was, and what the old woman had told him.

Slowly his eyes focused on the wooden bird on the shelf, the raven he had given Pappi. It seemed now that a different boy had painted it, a simpler and a younger boy. It had meant something to Pappi, then? Enough for him to slip it into his pocket before leaving? But . . . not enough to make him change his mind.

Tomas hadn't heard the old woman get up, but the curtains were pulled back and she was outside with her dog. When she came in she banged snow from her boots, and Fritzi jumped up to lick Tomas's face.

There was rabbit stew again for breakfast.

'Where now, boy?' the old woman asked as they ate.

He had hardly thought. 'I'll go back to the monastery,' he said now. 'Then home.'

'Where's home?'

He looked down. 'Unterberg.'

The old woman stared. 'Did you know my son, then? Niklas – Niklas Rust?'

'Only a little,' he said. Perhaps that was true.

'You'd better tell his wife what happened, then, if you see her, poor thing.'

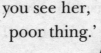

She was wrapping a piece of cooked rabbit in a cloth, and some dried berries.

He should tell *her*, shouldn't he? He opened his mouth, but the words 'You're my grandmother' dried up in his throat, crumbled to pieces and turned themselves into a cough.

The old woman held out the wrapped food. 'Here's something to eat later. Take care. Don't try to get up to the ridge. I'll show you the longer way round, by the track. It adds a few miles, but keep up a good pace and you'll be at the monastery by dusk.'

His jacket and cap were warming by the fire. He put them on, and laced his boots. The sky was clear, but out in the biting cold Tomas pulled his collar up and his cap down. They set off into the woods, the old woman pulling her sledge, Fritzi running ahead.

She stopped by a log pile. 'Now, you go along that way – through the clearing, past the tarn. There's a rough path through the trees. After a good few miles you'll come to the track that winds round and up to the monastery. Take care, now, and be sure to stick to that path.'

Tomas thanked her for her kindness and said goodbye. Fritzi ran with him a little way until the old woman whistled him back.

It felt dream-like, walking on alone. As if he was a different boy – a boy without a father. A boy whose father had gone for ever.

No father, but a new grandmother. He thought she must have something of his father's fearless spirit, to live alone in her hut through the harshness of winter.

He should have told her.

His path took him to the grave, and there he stopped.

He couldn't walk past.

He plucked a few holly berries and laid them on the mound. Then, as he stood looking, something built up inside him, pressing against his chest, and up to the top of his head, and in his throat. He didn't know whether to weep or shout.

It was shouting that burst out of him.

'I hate you, Pappi – *hate* you! You're a liar and a cheat! You didn't love us, did you? You only cared about yourself. Poor Mamma – did you think of her? Did you stop to think how it'd be – waiting and waiting for someone who was never coming back? And what about Johanna? Don't you think she needs a proper father? Don't you think *I* do? How could you leave us like that – how could you? We were – we were nuisances to you, just nuisances! You left us behind to start your new life without us. Only you haven't got a new life, have you? Niklas Rust, the brave mountaineer, the guide – what good did that do you? All the things you told me – all those warnings – what to do, what not to do, how to keep safe . . . *Now* look at you! I was always proud of you – didn't you know that? My big, brave father. And I want to be proud still. How can I be proud, though, how can I, when you're – when you're a cheat and a liar . . .'

The tears were winning after all. He knelt by the grave and wept. He wept for the father he loved. He wept for the father he had never really known, and now never would.

Footsteps crunched in the snow behind him. The old woman. He hadn't even thought that she'd hear him. He'd been shouting so loudly that she could hardly *not* have heard.

'Why didn't you tell me?' she said.

Fritzi gave a little whine and sat down in the snow.

'I – I didn't know how,' Tomas sobbed.

'Why didn't I guess?' Her hand was on his shoulder. 'Does your mother know you've come looking?'

'I left her a note.'

'Just a note?'

'Yes.' Tomas felt ashamed. He'd been nearly as bad as his father – walking out, without saying where he was going.

'Then,' said the old woman, 'you'd best get back to her, quick as you can. Tell her everything I've told you.'

Tomas got to his feet. She grasped his arm, helping him up, and kept hold.

'Never thought I'd meet my grandson. My eyes aren't good, but I see how like him you are.' She gazed at him, and raised a hand to touch his face. 'A fine brave boy. Tomas, you said? So you're Tomas Rust.'

'I am. And there's Johanna as well. My little sister. She's your granddaughter.'

The old woman's face creased into a smile. Tomas thought of his mother saying that Pappi was like sunshine in May. Now he saw it in his grandmother. He had never seen a smile of such delight, as if her face was brightly lit from inside.

'So I've got two beautiful grandchildren! I've lost my son, but I've found the two of you. Or at least you've found *me*.' She shook her head in wonderment. 'Whoever would have thought I could be so lucky?'

Tomas shifted his feet in the snow – wanting to stay, anxious to go.

The old woman sensed his mood. 'But you can't stand here talking, not with the days so short. You get on your way, then, Tomas, back to your mother. And go well. You know where to find me. Come back, won't you? Soon? Some day in summer, when the days are long and the weather fine. I'll be waiting.'

'I will,' he promised.

Chapter Thirteen:

Never Ever

Tomas was making good progress. With new energy after the rest and the hot food, he walked briskly. His mind was whirring.

It can't be true. It must be true, said the rhythm of his stride. *Must be true. Can't be true.*

He'd seen his father's grave. Met the person who'd seen him dead. What could be more certain that that?

Dead. Gone. Dead. Gone, said his steps.

Never. Ever. Never. Ever. Never see him again.

It was a fuzzing in his brain, a blurring of his eyes, a jibbing of his thoughts. The words jumbled into nonsense.

When he saw a craggy route up beside a stream, he hesitated. The easy track the old woman had told him to take was the long way to the monastery, winding slowly up the mountainside. If he took this quick way to the ridge, he'd save an hour or two.

He stood eyeing the footholds and handholds. Big, tempting slabs jutted out from the cliff-face.

It didn't look impossible. After all, he was still the son of Niklas Rust. His father wouldn't hesitate. He wouldn't take the easier, longer way.

But: *Never take chances,* said his father's voice. *Only a fool takes chances on the mountain.*

Go away. I'm not listening to you, Tomas answered it. *You don't deserve it, not now.*

And into his mind came Wilhelm Tell's son

Walter, standing perfectly still with the apple on his head, trusting his father. Walter was lucky. *His* father was worthy of trust.

Tomas adjusted his rucksack securely on his shoulders and began to climb.

It felt good, reaching for handholds, testing a rock with his foot. He could do it – he was fit and strong. He soon gained enough height to make his stomach clench when he looked down. The stream was only a small one but it flung itself from the summit and fell to the gorge, crashing on rocks far below.

Up here he was buffeted by wind. He stopped on a narrow ledge, barely wide enough for both feet. The waterfall was dizzying, plunging past him in a plume of white, droplets flying. Fine spray misted his face. He gazed up at the top of the ravine.

The mountains could trick you. They made you feel strong and capable one moment, weak and fearful the next.

And there was something he hadn't thought of. What had made his father fall? Strong and experienced as he was? Could the Brockenspectre have startled him? Made him move clumsily, triggering the rock fall?

If the Brockenspectre loomed at you in a place like this, you'd be trapped in the narrow gorge. There'd be no escape. Only if you stepped out into air and let yourself fall—

Cra-aaarck!

Tomas's head whipped round. One foot skidded off the ledge and waved out into space. For a giddying moment he thought he'd summoned the Brockenspectre by thinking of it.

He scrabbled wildly, then wedged his hand into a crack and got control of his flailing foot.

When he was secure, he turned his head slowly.

Not a terrifying shadowy figure, but a large brown bird that glided away, riding the wind. Eagle, perhaps, or buzzard. It had flown so close that its wing-beats fanned his face. He must have surprised it where it perched.

He stood gasping, his heart thumping loudly. Somehow he hadn't fallen. Somehow he was still clinging to the rock.

Keep your head, said his father. *Always keep a clear head.*

He breathed hard, and carried on climbing. His hands were frozen, his movements clumsy.

You need only make one mistake. He'd already had one fall. He couldn't be so lucky twice.

He made himself climb slowly, carefully, testing each hold. At last he heaved himself over a boulder, and was on level ground.

The ridge! He was on the ridge at last. He was weak with relief, feeling the rasp of his breath, the tremor in his legs.

Good boy, said his father's voice – so close that Tomas looked round, almost expecting to see him. But he was alone in the mist, and snow was starting to fall.

If he'd slipped and fallen to the rocks –

His mother would wait and wait for him at home, not knowing.

He must get back to her.

Tomas walked on fast, banging his sides to warm himself.

Monastery

When storms rage, I am here.

When fog shrouds the mountains, I am here.

When lightning strikes, when ice holds fast, when torrents are loosed, I am here.

When armies clash, when nations war, when rivals feud, I am here.

My cloisters embrace you.

My quietness calms your fears; my calmness quiets your anger.

My gentleness eases your loss; my prayers soothe your soul.

Come. I am here.

You bring nothing new.

No loss that has not been mourned a thousandfold.

No sorrow, no guilt, no failing that has not been keenly felt.

The joys and pains you feel so sharply are shared

by humankind.

When you are gone, others will come, and others, through all time.

Always and always I am here.

Chapter Fourteen:

Above the Clouds

The monastery loomed into view, dark and huge in the fading light. As before, Tomas let himself through the iron gates.

He was tempted to sleep with Bruno again, keeping hidden. Glancing into the stable, though, he found it empty – maybe it wasn't late enough for him to be shut in for the night. And Tomas had eaten the food the old woman had given him. Hunger took him to the front door. He mounted the steps and knocked loudly.

A bolt screeched back, a heavy fastening clanked, and the door opened. A monk in a belted black robe stood there. Tomas was surprised to see that he was a young man – he'd thought all monks were old.

'Welcome to this place.' The monk held his hands as if praying, and bowed his head.

'Can I stay here tonight?'

'Of course. Please come in.'

Tomas did so, and entered a place of warmth and candle-flame, ancient stone and flickering light. He let himself sink into its welcome. The loneliness and dangers of his journey dropped away as his hands and feet began to thaw.

The young monk guided him to a large refectory, with tables and benches and a fire burning in the grate, throwing out warmth. Another fetched him a meal of soup, bread and cheese while the first went to see about a bed. Then, as Tomas finished eating, a third monk, an older man, came and sat at the table opposite him.

'I am Brother Gerard. You are welcome here.'

'Thank you,' said Tomas shyly.

Brother Gerard had a kind, wrinkled face and bright brown eyes behind round spectacles. 'You're young to be out alone – where are you bound?' he asked.

'Home, to Unterberg.'

'What has brought you here?'

'I was looking for my father. I think you know – knew – him. His name is – his name was – Niklas Rust.'

'Ah!' the monk exclaimed. 'You are Tomas? Tomas Rust?'

Tomas nodded.

'Then – people are looking for *you*,' said Brother Gerard. 'Max Oberlin, the carpenter, was here yesterday. Your mother is sick with worry, he said. But now here you are, fit and well.'

Tomas felt bad. 'I'll get home tomorrow as soon as I can.'

'Yes, you must,' said the monk. 'We were sad here to learn that your father was missing. We know him well. He's helped us here with many a rescue. Such a brave man. Always willing to go out in the worst weather if someone needed help. The brothers have searched for him, and sought information, but have found nothing.'

'He's dead,' Tomas blurted, and he told the shocked monk what he'd learned.

He was sobbing again by the end, when he told Brother Gerard how he'd shouted and yelled by the grave. 'I said I hated him! But I don't really. I wanted to trust him. Now everything's spoiled. He didn't want us. He left us behind.'

'But who's to say,' said Brother Gerard, 'that he wouldn't have changed his mind, and come back to you? We have no way of knowing, since the poor man met his death, God rest his soul.'

He kept the painted raven I gave him, Tomas

remembered. *He took it with him. He wanted something to keep.*

'You must try to remember his qualities,' said Brother Gerard, 'and find them in yourself.'

'His qualities?' Tomas wiped his eyes. 'He was a cheat and a liar.'

Brother Gerard nodded. 'He was false and true. He was foolish and wise. He was cowardly and brave. He was all those things, as most of us are. And don't forget your other parent! You're not only your father's son, are you? There's your mother. What do you get from her?'

Tomas looked at him, not sure how to answer.

'What are the good things about your mother?' the monk prompted.

'Well – she's kind,' said Tomas, thinking. 'Always. And gentle.

And skilful. And she works very hard.'

'Patient, too, I don't doubt. And reliable. And lots more besides. Now, I can see you're drooping with tiredness. Let's find you a bed.'

Tomas was woken before dawn next morning by the sounds of the monks rising for prayers. He heard their hushed voices, and the soft tread of sandals on stone floor as they moved off towards the chapel.

Half of him felt sorry to leave this calm, orderly place, but the other half was anxious to return to Mamma. He thought of the note he'd left, and how worried she'd have been. How much he'd have to tell her!

There would be hard, hard things for her to learn.

First, though, he must complete his journey.

When the monks had finished their prayers, he joined them for a simple breakfast. As Tomas had expected, Brother Gerard was unwilling to let him finish his journey alone.

'I wish I could go with you, Tomas. My knees aren't what they were and I struggle on the slopes, but I'll ask one of the younger brothers to walk with you.'

'Thank you, but . . . I want to go by myself.'

Brother Gerard shook his head. 'We both know the dangers. One slip, that's all it takes. You don't need me to tell you that.'

'Please! It's important.' Tomas was just as determined. 'I've come so far by myself and now there's just this last bit.'

'Yes. I can understand that,' said Brother Gerard. 'But I'd never forgive myself if you met with an accident.'

Then Tomas thought of a solution.

'Could Bruno come with me? I'd be safe with him. When I get down to the trees, and the track to the village, I could send him back. He knows the way.'

'Hmm,' said Brother Gerard, and smiled. 'I can see you're the son of Niklas Rust. Well, I suppose so. And the weather's fair today. But you must take great care.'

Tomas strode easily, Bruno loping beside him. It was good to have a dog for company. Maybe he'd ask Mamma if they could have a dog of their own – not a huge one like Bruno, who'd take a lot of feeding, but a more ordinary dog like Fritzi. A dog full of energy and cheerfulness.

Already Tomas knew that he would come to the mountains again and again. The mountains stirred something in his soul. He would learn their ways, their moods, their secrets.

He and Karl could walk together, proper friends again. He imagined them striding along the ridge, a black-and-white dog leaping ahead.

The light today was strange, in a way Tomas hadn't seen before. Dense cloud lingered in the valley, while the mountain tops were in low, dramatic sunlight that slanted over the high peaks. He was looking down on a blanket of cloud so thick and level that he imagined walking on it. His journey would take him down into that gloom, and he thought of people in the valleys not knowing that the high tops were brilliant with sunshine.

The air was still and cold. Walking across a low ridge, he paused to see where his path led.

Then he saw something that made his heart thud in fear.

Below him, on the cloud –

The massive figure of a man.

A giant. A huge, shadowy giant. And a great bear-like creature beside him.

Tomas stood shocked and still. The Brockenspectre. It must be! He'd almost forgotten. Had he come so far, only to fall victim to the Brockenspectre on the last stage of his journey?

His heart was thumping.

But his fear lasted only for a second, replaced by wonder as he gazed at the phantom figure. Rainbow colours played around its head, like a halo.

Where had it come from? He had expected to meet it up in the heights, not below him, lying on a cloud as if floating there.

The Brockenspectre. *Here* at last was the Brockenspectre.

A figure to haunt, to astound – but not terrify.

It was a figure of eeriness and strangeness, but also of beauty.

Then he realized. He raised an arm, and the Brockenspectre raised an arm, too, waving back.

'Look, Bruno! Look!' Tomas knelt to cuddle the dog, and below him man and bear became a single shape.

This was what Pappi had seen. This was what Pappi had described. Not a monster, not an enemy – he had seen his own shadow, magnified and huge. Just as Tomas was seeing his own shadow now.

Brockenspectre

I am your giant, rarely seen; I am your self made magnificent.

Stand and wonder at my size, my splendour.

I hang in haze, float above chasms; I bestride the mountain.

Caught sunlight haloes my head.

I am your ghost, your phantom, your spectre.

No more can you catch me than trap a cloud, snare a sunbeam, snatch a speeding swallow.

Do not tremble.

Fear me only as you fear yourself.

I am as dark as your fears, airy as your hopes.

Heavy as your sorrows, light as your joys.

I am you.

Chapter Fifteen:
Home

Reluctant to leave his giant companion, Tomas walked slowly down the crest of the ridge. The Brockenspectre moved with him, fading as the path lost height. Soon the massive figure had melted into mist.

Tomas and Bruno made their way down the rocky path. Lower down, where the hillsides were clad in cloud, Tomas looked back and had a sense of golden haze above him, where sunlight warmed the uplands. If he wanted, he could retrace his steps, and burst into it, like a surfacing swimmer taking gulps of air. The Brockenspectre, his other, stronger self, would be there to greet him.

It felt wondrous. The sighting of his shadow double had filled him with strength. He knew that a part of him would always belong to the mountains. Wherever he went, the mountains would pull him back.

He was his father's son. Yes, and his mother's son, too. He was Tomas Rust.

Now that he could see his path down to the village, it was time for a sad parting.

'Goodbye, Bruno. You can go back now. Thank you! I'll come and see you soon.'

He buried his face in the dog's thick fur, then stood and pointed upwards. 'Home! Go home!'

Bruno gazed at him, then whuffed in understanding, and padded off. Tomas watched him until he reached a brow of hill. Bruno looked back at him once, then turned and was gone.

The mist was not so thick as to obscure the path, and Tomas's progress was sure and steady.

He'd been away for only three nights, but felt as if he'd been on an immensely long journey, and was returning as a different, changed person – bigger, stronger. He strode out, feeling that he could walk on for many a mile if he had to.

Soon, threading his way between thickets of birch and pine, he saw Unterberg below him: its church spire reaching for the sky, its houses clustered. The grass was all silvered over with frost that crunched under his boots as he walked. The trees held out ghostly arms, and the fine twigs were like clouds.

It would soon be winter, and the snows would come. The village would huddle into itself, cut off from the valley below. The villagers would fetch in wood, carry hay and water for their animals, close their shutters against the long, dark nights, and warm themselves by their fires.

The light was fading fast as he left the glacier path and reached the village street. Lamps were lit in the windows of the Alpenrose Inn, and he heard voices inside, and someone playing an accordion. He wondered if Karl was there. He couldn't stop to see Karl now, though he had much to tell him. That must wait till tomorrow.

He walked on towards home.

Outside the cottage, he saw a group of figures: Mamma, and little Johanna. And Max, who was either coming or going, the way he often did seem to be coming or going. Tomas stood for a moment and took a deep breath.

Kind, reliable Max. Good. Mamma would need him now.

She was holding Johanna's hand, about to go inside. Then she turned, and saw Tomas coming down the lane. She held a hand to her throat.

'Oh! Tommi, Tom, is it you?' She stood in shock for a moment, then rushed to him, arms outstretched. 'I thought for a moment you were Niklas – but Tomas, it really is you! You've come back! Oh, I've been so worried . . .'

Max had lifted Johanna onto his shoulders,
and was coming along more slowly. 'Tommi!
Tommi!' she squealed.

Tomas laughed, and went to meet them. He
let himself be fussed over, and given a hero's
welcome.

He was home.

AUTHOR'S NOTE

Are you wondering about the name Brockenspectre? It comes from the Harz Mountains in Germany, where one of the peaks is called the Brocken. The light there often produces the right conditions for walkers to see their own shadow figure on clouds below. Because of their strange, ghostly appearance, these figures have come to be known as Brockenspectres.

I've never seen one; not yet. Once, though, in an aeroplane, I looked out of the window and glimpsed the haloed shadow of the aircraft on clouds below. My father saw this, too, during his RAF days, and he learned the name Brockenspectre. He told me about it, years ago; I liked the word, and it stayed in my mind. This story grew from there.

Thanks, as always, to David Fickling, Bella Pearson and Linda Sargent for their guidance and encouragement, to Trevor Arrowsmith for support (especially cooking), and to Pam Smy, without whose wonderful illustrations this would be only half the book it is.

Hidden at the end of Grandpa's garden,
Lucy has a magical secret . . .

LOB

Linda Newbery

By the winner of the **Costa Children's Book Prize**

He's older than anyone can tell.
Older than the trees.
Older than anybody.

Linda Newbery, with the vivid embroidery of
Pam Smy's illustrations, has conjured a real green
man right out of the woods and stories of legend.

Turn over to read an extract from this enchanting story.

Early June

'Lob?' said Grandpa Will, in the summer garden. 'Oh, he's older than anyone can tell. Older than the trees. Older than anybody.'

'And what does he do?' asked Lucy. She knew the answer, but liked Grandpa to tell her.

'Lob-work, that's what he does. Odd jobs around the place.' He always said it like that – Lob-work. Whenever he and Lucy were out here, Grandpa would look at a well-tended onion bed, or a watering can filled and ready, and he'd smile. And sometimes he'd look towards the hedge, as if someone was there. When Lucy looked too, she'd see only a quiver in the leaves; a mouse,

perhaps, or a spider. The thing about Lob
was that not everyone could see him. Most
people couldn't.

'How long has Lob been here?' Lucy
asked. She knew the story, but liked hearing
it over and over again.

'Oh, a long, long time. Long before you
were born. Before your dad was born,'

Grandpa said, his voice settling comfortably into the telling. 'It was just after your gran and I got married, and came to live here. I was chopping wood one evening, when all of a sudden I knew I was being watched. So I stopped chopping and turned round. In the corner of my eye I saw him. There he stood' – he turned round to look – 'just there, by the bench. But I could only see him side-long. When I stared straight at him, he faded away. Still, I knew who he was, knew at once. I'd heard about Lob from my grandfather, and he'd heard from *his* grandfather, and so on, back and back and back. There's always been Lob. He walks the roads, that's what he does. He walks and he walks, and he looks for the right person. When he finds that person, he stays around for a very long time. So I hoped he'd stay with me, and when he did I knew how lucky I was.'

'Lob chose you!'

'He did.'

'Will he always stay?'

'Till I die, I hope,' said Grandpa, looking round as if he wanted Lob to hear.

'But you're not going to die, are you, Grandpa?'

'We all will, in the end,' Grandpa said. 'But we needn't worry ourselves. I'm not expecting it for a while yet.'

They walked down to the end of the vegetable garden. Just the two of them, or perhaps it was the three of them.

'Is he here now?' Lucy asked, peering into the thicket of raspberry canes. 'Can you see him?'

'He'll be around somewhere. He don't always choose to be seen, Lob doesn't.'

'Will I see him?'

'I wouldn't be at all surprised,' said Grandpa. 'You're good at seeing.'

Lucy wanted and wanted and wanted to

be a Lob person. She squeezed her hands into fists with wanting; she clenched her eyes tight shut, and hoped that Lob would be there when she opened them.

He wasn't. But she was sure that one day he would be.

The others – Mum and Dad and Granny Annie – thought Lob was just a game, though Grandpa often mentioned him.

'It's lucky I've got Lob,' Grandpa would say, sitting down on the bench for a rest. 'I'd find it all a bit much, these days.' And always he said, 'Thank you, my friend' – first thing in the morning, and every time he finished work and went indoors.

'Don't fill the child's head with your nonsense!' Granny would tell him, tutting. And she'd look at Lucy and shake her head, smiling, as if Lucy was old enough to know better, and Grandpa was the child.

Whatever the grown-ups said, Lucy knew there was special magic here.

She knew it whenever she came to Granny and Grandpa's. On summer mornings, early, when the grass glittered with dew. On winter nights, looking through the window of her attic room. The darkness out there was giddy with stars, and she heard the cry of an owl, or a fox, or a something, from down in the woods.

Garden magic tingled through her, from her hair to her toe-nails.

Mum said that the magic was in Grandpa's fingers. Green fingers, Mum said he had. And Lucy giggled, imagining Grandpa with green pointy fingers like an elf. In fact his hands were square and stubby, with tough, cracked nails, from all the garden work he did. He had to do a lot of scrubbing to get his hands clean when he came indoors.

Every day, Grandpa Will worked on his vegetable patch. He grew peas and runner beans, raspberries and gooseberries, carrots and parsnips, lettuces and onions and

potatoes: all in neat rows, in beds that were perfectly dug and weeded.

It was a lot for him to do, all by himself. But of course, according to Grandpa, he didn't do it on his own; he was helped by Lob, in all sorts of ways. When Lob wasn't skittering about the woods or sleeping in the hedge, he found jobs to do. He collected logs, swept up piles of leaves, cleaned the tools, weeded the beds and picked off slugs and snails.

Lob only did it when no one was looking, Grandpa said. And only when he wanted.

'You can't give him orders, tell him what to do,' Grandpa told Lucy. 'He does what he likes, Lob does.'

Often, Lucy tried to spy on Lob, hoping for just a glimpse. She'd dart out of the back door, or stalk round the corner of the cottage. But she'd never seen him, no matter how hard she searched or how cold she got, lurking in wait.

It was the beginning of June. The sky stretched high and higher, streaked with cloud. Lucy and Grandpa Will were down in the garden, planting out runner beans. These leafy little plants had grown from the beans they'd sown in small pots, last time Lucy stayed. That was magic, if anything was!